Samuel Taylor Coleridge

So this then is ye Rime of ye ancient mariner

Samuel Taylor Coleridge

So this then is ye Rime of ye ancient mariner

ISBN/EAN: 9783337174743

Printed in Europe, USA, Canada, Australia, Japan

Cover: Foto ©Andreas Hilbeck / pixelio.de

More available books at **www.hansebooks.com**

SO THIS THEN IS YE

RIME

of ye

ANCIENT MARINER

WHEREIN

Is told Whilom on a Day an Ancient Sea-Faring Man Detaineth a Wedding-Guest & Telleth him a Grewsome Tale.

Written by *SAMVEL TAYLOR COLE-RIDGE*

For ye better Understanding of ye Gentle Reader, Various Pictures are here Inserted by one *William W. Denslow*

Ye First Edition Corrected and Improved

Done into a Booke by ye merrie ROYCROFTERS at ye *ROY-CROFT SHOP*, at ye Sign of ye *Hippocampus*, adjacent to ye Deestrick Academy for ye Younge, which is in *East Aurora*, New York, United States of America. *1899*

Of this edition there were printed but Nine Hundred and Ten copies and types were then distributed. This book is No.

Various of ye pictures are did by hande by ye *First Ladies* of East Aurora at a Bee : where· ye Ladies were kindly supervised by ye DEACON DENSLOW.

PART ONE

YE RIME of ye ANCIENT MARINER

PART I.

T is an ancient Mar-
iner,
And he stoppeth
one of three.
“By thy long gray beard and
glittering eye,
Now wherefore stopp'st thou
me?

An ancient Mariner meeteth three gallants bidden to a wedding feast, and detaineth one.

"The Bridegroom's doors are opened wide,
And I am next of kin;
The guests are met, the feast is set;
May'st hear the merry din."

He holds him with his skinny hand;
"There was a ship," quoth he.
"Hold off! unhand me, gray-beard loon!"
Eftsoons his hand dropt he.

The Wedding-Guest is spell-bound by

He holds him with his glittering eye;

The Wedding-Guest stood still,
And listens like a three years' child;
The Mariner hath his will.

the eye of the old seafaring man, and constrained to hear his tale.

The Wedding-Guest sat on a stone:
He cannot choose but hear;
And thus spake on that ancient man,
The bright-eyed Mariner:

"The ship was cheered, the harbor cleared,
Merrily did we drop
Below the kirk, below the hill,
Below the lighthouse top.

The Mariner telleth how the ship sailed southward with a good wind and fair weather, till it reached the Line.

"The sun came up upon the left,
Out of the sea came he;
And he shone bright, and on the right
Went down into the sea.

"Higher and higher every day,
Till over the mast at noon—"
The Wedding-Guest here beat his breast,
For he heard the loud bassoon.

The Wedding-Guest heareth the bridal

The bride hath paced into the hall,
Red as a rose is she;

Nodding their heads before her goes
The merry minstrelsy.

music; but the Mariner continueth his tale.

The Wedding-Guest here beat his breast,
Yet he cannot choose but hear;
And thus spake on that ancient man,
The bright-eyed Mariner:

"And now the storm-blast came, and he
Was tyrannous and strong:
He struck with his o'ertaking wings,
And chased us south along.

The ship drawn by a storm toward the south pole.

"With sloping masts and dipping
prow,
As who pursued with yell & blow
Still treads the shadow of his foe,
And forward bends his head,
The ship drove fast, loud roared
the blast,
And southward aye we fled.

"And now there came both mist
and snow,
And it grew wondrous cold:
And ice, mast-high, came floating by,
As green as emerald.

"And through the drifts the
snowy clifts
Did send a dismal sheen:
Nor shapes of men nor beasts
we ken,—
The ice was all between.

The land of ice, and of fearful sound where no living being was to be seen.

"The ice was here, the ice was
there,
The ice was all around:
It cracked and growled, and
roared and howled,
Like noises in a swound!

"At length did cross an Albatross;
Through the fog it came;

Till a great sea-bird, called the Albatross, came through the snow-fog and was received with great joy and hospitality.

As if it had been a Christian
soul,
We hailed it in God's name.

"It ate the food it ne'er had eat,
And round and round it flew.
The ice did split with a thunder-
fit;
The helmsman steered us
through!

And lo! the Albatross proveth a bird of good omen, and followeth the ship as it returned northward through fog and floating ice.

"And a good south-wind sprung
up behind;
The Albatross did follow,
And every day, for food or play,
Came to the mariners' hollo!

"In mist or cloud, on mast or
shroud,
It perched for vespers nine;
Whiles all the night, through
fog-smoke white,
Glimmered the white moon-
shine."

"God save thee, ancient Mariner!
From the fiends, that plague
thee thus!—
Why look'st thou so!"—"With
my cross-bow
I shot the Albatross!"

The ancient Mariner inhospitably killeth the pious bird of good omen.

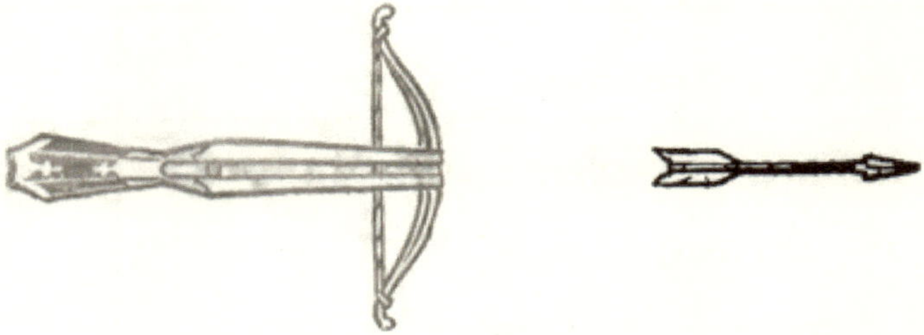

PART TWO

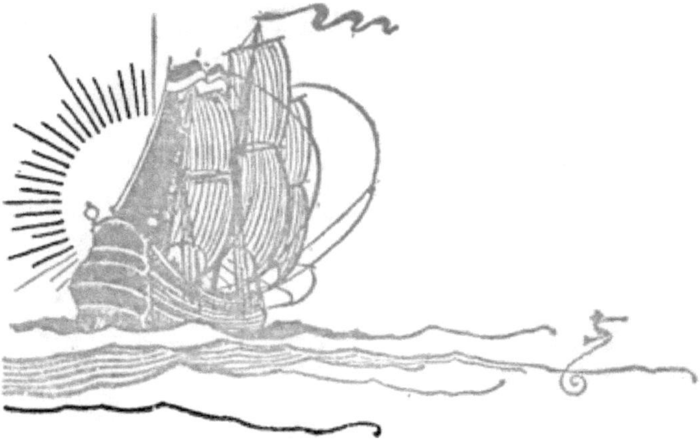

PART II.

THE sun now rose
upon the right:
Out of the sea
came he,
Still hid in mist, and on the left
Went down into the sea.

And the good south-wind still
blew behind,
But no sweet bird did follow,
Nor any day for food or play
Came to the mariners' hollo!

His shipmates cry out against the ancient Mariner, for killing the bird of good luck.

And I had done a hellish thing,
And it would work 'em woe:
For all averred, I had killed the bird
That made the breeze to blow.
Ah, wretch! said they, the bird to slay,
That made the breeze to blow!

But when the fog cleared off, they justify the same, and thus make themselves accomplices in the crime.

Nor dim nor red, like God's own head,
The glorious sun uprist:
Then all averred, I had killed the bird
That brought the fog and mist.

'T was right, said they, such
birds to slay,
That bring the fog and mist.

The fair breeze blew, the white
foam flew,
The furrow followed free;
We were the first that ever burst
Into that silent sea.

The fair breeze continues; the ship enters the Pacific Ocean, and sails northward, even till it reached the Line.

Down dropt the breeze, the sails
dropt down.
'T was sad as sad could be:
And we did speak only to break
The silence of the sea!

The ship hath been suddenly becalmed.

All in a hot and copper sky,
The bloody sun, at noon,
Right up above the mast did
stand,
No bigger than the moon.

Day after day, day after day,
We stuck, nor breath nor mo-
tion;
As idle as a painted ship
Upon a painted ocean.

And the Albatross begins to be avenged.

Water, water, everywhere,
And all the boards did shrink;
Water, water, everywhere,
Nor any drop to drink.

The very deep did rot: O Christ!
That ever this should be!
Yea, slimy things did crawl with
legs
Upon the slimy sea.

About, about, in reel and rout
The death-fires danced at night;
The water, like a witch's oils,
Burnt green, and blue, and
white.

And some in dreams assured
were
Of the spirit that plagued us so;

A Spirit had followed them; one of the invisible inhabitants of this planet, neither departed souls nor angels; concerning whom the learned Jew, Josephus, and the Platonic Constantinopolitan, Michael Psellus, may be consulted. They are very numerous, and there is no climate or element without one or more.

Nine fathoms deep he had followed us
From the land of mist and snow.

And every tongue, through utter drought,
Was withered at the root;
We could not speak, no more than if
We had been choked with soot.

The shipmates, in their sore distress, would fain throw the whole guilt on the ancient Mariner: in sign whereof they hang the dead sea-bird round his neck.

Ah! well-a-day! what evil looks
Had I from old and young!
Instead of the cross, the Albatross
About my neck was hung.

PART THREE

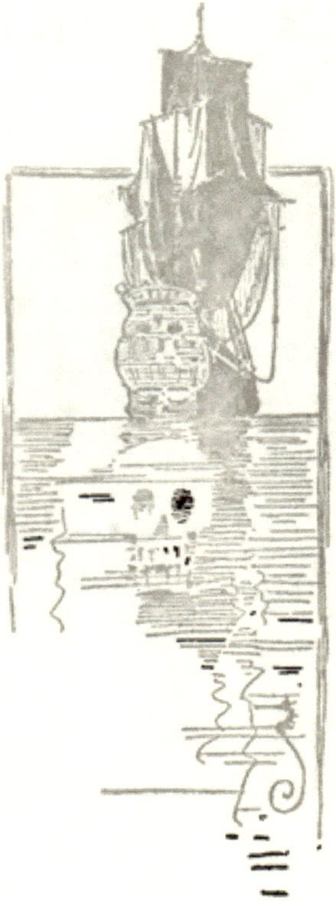

PART III.

THERE passed a weary time. Each throat
Was parched, and glazed each eye.
When looking westward, I beheld
A something in the sky.

The ancient Mariner beholdeth a sign in the element afar off.

At first it seemed a little speck,
And then it seemed a mist;

It moved and moved, and took
at last
A certain shape, I wist.

A speck, a mist, a shape, I wist!
And still it neared and neared:
As if it dodged a water-sprite,
It plunged and tacked and
veered.

At its nearer approach, it seemeth him to be a ship; and at a dear ransom he freeth his speech from the bonds of thirst.

With throats unslaked, with
black lips baked,
We could nor laugh nor wail;
Through utter drought all
dumb we stood!
I bit my arm, I sucked the blood,
And cried, A sail, A sail!

With throats unslaked, with
black lips baked,
Agape they heard me call:
Grammercy! they for joy did
grin,
And all at once their breath
drew in,
As they were drinking all.

A flash of joy;

See! see! (I cried) she tacks
no more!
Hither to work us weal,—
Without a breeze, without a tide,
She steadies with upright keel!

And horror follows. For can it be a ship that comes onward without wind or tide?

The western wave was all aflame,
The day was wellnigh done!

Almost upon the western wave
Rested the broad bright sun;
When that strange shape drove
suddenly
Betwixt us and the sun.

It seemeth him but the skeleton of a ship.

And straight the sun was fleck-
ed with bars,
(Heaven's Mother send us
grace!)
As if through a dungeon-grate
he peered
With broad and burning face.

Alas! (thought I, and my heart
beat loud)
How fast she nears and nears!

Are those her sails that glance
in the sun,
Like restless gossameres?

Are those her ribs through which
the sun
Did peer, as through a grate?
And is that woman all her crew?
Is that a Death? and are there
two?
Is Death that Woman's mate?

And its ribs are seen as bars on the face of the setting sun. The Spectre Woman and her Death-mate, and no other on board the skeleton-ship.

Her lips were red, her looks
were free,
Her locks were yellow as gold:
Her skin was as white as leprosy,

Like vessel, like crew!

The Nightmare Life-in-Death
was she,
Who thicks man's blood with
cold.

Death and Life-in-Death have diced for the ship's crew, and she (the latter) winneth the ancient Mariner.

The naked hulk alongside came,
And the twain were casting dice?
"The game is done! I've won!
I've won!"
Quoth she, and whistles thrice.

No twilight within the courts of the sun.

The sun's rim dips; the stars
rush out:
At one stride comes the dark;
With far-heard whisper, o'er the
sea,
Off shot the spectre-bark.

We listened and looked side-
ways up!
Fear at my heart, as at a cup,
My life-blood seemed to sip!
The stars were dim, and thick
the night,
The steersman's face by his lamp
gleamed white;

From the sails the dew did
drip,—
Till clomb above the eastern bar
The horned moon, with one
bright star
Within the nether tip.

One after one, by the star-
dogged moon,

At the rising of the moon.

One after another,

Too quick for groan or sigh,
Each turned his face with a
ghastly pang,
And cursed me with his eye.

His shipmates drop down dead.

Four times fifty living men,
(And I heard nor sigh nor
groan!)
With heavy thump, a lifeless
lump,
They dropped down one by one.

But Life-in-Death begins her work on the ancient Mariner.

The souls did from their bodies
fly,—
They fled to bliss or woe!
And every soul, it passed me by,
Like the whizz of my cross-bow!

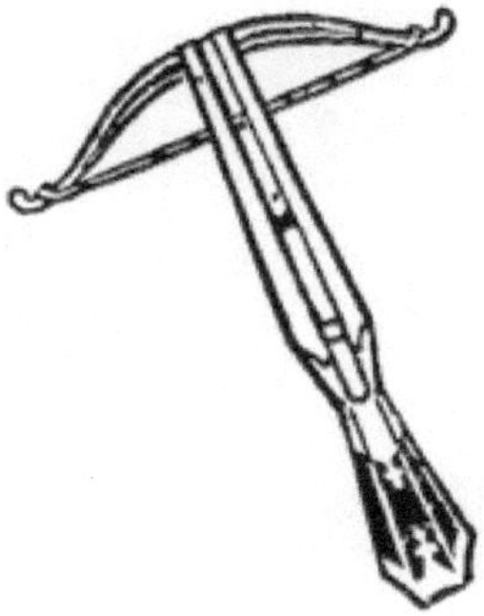

PART FOUR

PART IV.

"I FEAR thee, ancient Mariner!
I fear thy skinny hand!
And thou art long, and lank, and brown,
As is the ribbed sea-sand.

I fear thee & thy glittering eye,
And thy skinny hand, so brown."—

The Wedding-Guest feareth that a Spirit is talking to him.

But the ancient Mariner assureth him of his bodily life, and proceedeth to relate his horrible penance.

"Fear not, fear not, thou Wedding-Guest!
This body dropt not down.

Alone, alone, all, all alone,
Alone on a wide, wide sea!
And never a saint took pity on
My soul in agony.

He despiseth the creatures of the calm.

The many men, so beautiful!
And they all dead did lie:
And a thousand thousand slimy things
Lived on; and so did I.

And envieth that they should

I looked upon the rotting sea,
And drew my eyes away;

I looked upon the rotting deck,
And there the dead men lay.

live, and so many lie dead.

I looked to heaven, and tried
to pray;
But or ever a prayer had gusht,
A wicked whisper came, and
made
My heart as dry as dust.

I closed my lids, and kept them
close,
And the balls like pulses beat;
For the sky and the sea, and
the sea and the sky
Lay like a load on my weary
eye,
And the dead were at my feet.

But the curse liveth for him in the eye of the dead men.

The cold sweat melted from
their limbs,
Nor rot nor reek did they:
The look with which they look-
ed on me
Had never passed away.

An orphan's curse would drag
to hell
A spirit from on high;
But oh! more horrible than that
Is the curse in a dead man's eye!
Seven days, seven nights, I saw
that curse,
And yet I could not die.

The moving Moon went up
the sky,
And nowhere did abide:
Softly she was going up,
And a star or two beside—

Her beams bemocked the sul-
try main,
Like April hoar-frost spread;
But where the ship's huge shad-
ow lay,
The charmed water burnt alway
A still and awful red.

Beyond the shadow of the ship,
I watched the water-snakes:
They moved in tracks of shin-
ing white,

In his loneliness and fixedness he yearneth towards the journeying Moon, and the stars that still sojourn, yet still move onward; and everywhere the blue sky belongs to them, and is their appointed rest, and their native country and their own natural homes, which they enter unannounced, as lords that are certainly expected, and yet there is a silent joy at their arrival.

By the light of the moon he beholdeth God's creatures of the great calm.

And when they reared, the elfish light
Fell off in hoary flakes.

Within the shadow of the ship
I watched their rich attire:
Blue, glossy green, and velvet black,
They coiled and swam; and every track
Was a flash of golden fire.

Their beauty and their happiness.

O happy living things! no tongue
Their beauty might declare:
A spring of love gushed from my heart,

And I blessed them unaware,—
Sure my kind saint took pity
on me,
And I blessed them unaware.

He blesseth them in his heart.

The selfsame moment I could
pray;
And from my neck so free
The Albatross fell off, and sank
Like lead into the sea."

The spell begins to break.

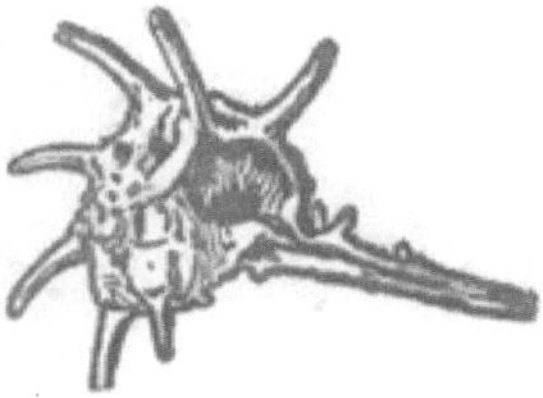

PART FIVE

PART V.

O SLEEP! it is a
gentle thing,
Beloved from pole
to pole!
To Mary Queen the praise be
given!
She sent the gentle sleep from
Heaven,
That slid into my soul.

The silly buckets on the deck,
That had so long remained,

By grace of the holy Mother,

the ancient Mariner is refreshed with rain.

I dreamt that they were filled
with dew;
And when I awoke, it rained.

My lips were wet, my throat
was cold,
My garments all were dank;
Sure I had drunken in my
dreams.
And still my body drank.

I moved, and could not feel my
limbs:
I was so light—almost
I thought that I had died in
sleep,
And was a blessed ghost.

He heareth sounds and seeth strange sights and commotions in the sky and the element.

And soon I heard a roaring
wind:
It did not come anear;
But with its sound it shook the
sails,
That were so thin and sere.

The upper air burst into life!
And a hundred fire-flags sheen,
To and fro they were hurried
about!
And to and fro, and in and out,
The wan stars danced between.

And the coming wind did roar
more loud,
And the sails did sigh like sedge;

And the rain poured down from
 one black cloud;
The moon was at its edge.

The thick black cloud was cleft,
 and still
The moon was at its side:
Like waters shot from some high
 crag,
The lightning fell with never a
 jag,
A river steep and wide.

The bodies of the ship's crew are inspired, and the ship moves on;

The loud wind never reached
 the ship,
Yet now the ship moved on!

Beneath the lightning and the
moon
The dead men gave a groan.

They groaned, they stirred, they
all uprose,
Nor spake, nor moved their eyes;
It had been strange, even in a
dream,
To have seen those dead men
rise.

The helmsman steered, the ship
moved on;
Yet never a breeze up blew;
The mariners all 'gan work the
ropes,

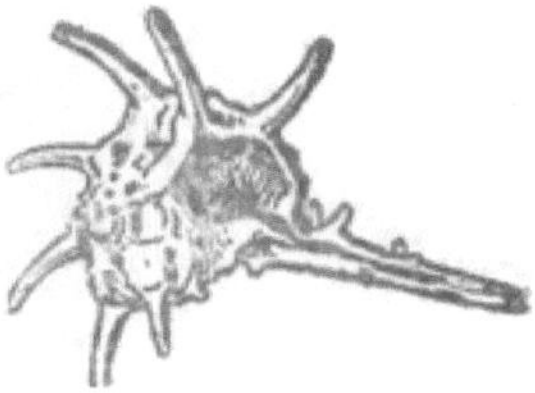

Where they were wont to do;
They raised their limbs like
lifeless tools,—
We were a ghastly crew.

The body of my brother's son
Stood by me, knee to knee:
The body and I pulled at one
rope,
But he said naught to me."

But not by the souls of the men, nor by demons of earth or middle air, but by a blessed troop of angelic spirits, sent down by the

"I fear thee, ancient Mariner!"
"Be calm, thou Wedding-Guest!
'T was not those souls that fled
in pain,
Which to their corses came again,
But a troop of spirits blest:

For when it dawned they dropped their arms,
And clustered round the mast;
Sweet sounds rose slowly through their mouths,
And from their bodies passed.

Around, around, flew each sweet sound,
Then darted to the sun;
Slowly the sounds came back again,
Now mixed, now one by one.

Sometimes a-dropping from the sky
I heard the skylark sing:

invocation of the guardian saint.

Sometimes all little birds that
are,
How they seemed to fill the
sea and air
With their sweet jargoning !

And now 't was like all instru-
ments,
Now like a lonely flute ;
And now it is an angel's song,
That makes the heavens be mute.

It ceased ; yet still the sails
made on
A pleasant noise till noon,
A noise like of a hidden brook
In the leafy month of June,

That to the sleeping woods all
night
Singeth a quiet tune.

Till noon we quietly sailed on,
Yet never a breeze did breathe:
Slowly and smoothly went the
ship,
Moved onward from beneath.

Under the keel nine fathom
deep,
From the land of mist and snow,
The Spirit slid: and it was he
That made the ship to go.
The sails at noon left off their
tune,
And the ship stood still also.

The lonesome Spirit from the South Pole carries on the ship as far as the Line, in obedience to the angelic troop, but still requireth vengeance.

The sun right up above the
mast,
Had fixed her to the ocean:
But in a minute she 'gan stir,
With a short uneasy motion,—
Backwards and forwards half
her length,
With a short uneasy motion.

Then like a pawing horse let go,
She made a sudden bound:
It flung the blood into my head,
As I fell down in a swound.

The Polar Spirit's fellow demons, the invisible inhabitants

How long in that same fit I lay,
I have not to declare;
But ere my living life returned,

I heard, and in my soul dis-
cerned
Two voices in the air.

'Is it he?' quoth one, 'Is this
the man?
By him who died on cross,
With his cruel bow he laid full low
The harmless Albatross.

The Spirit who abideth by him-
self
In the land of mist and snow,
He loved the bird that loved
the man
Who shot him with his bow.'

of the element, take part in his wrong; and two of them relate, one to the other, that penance long and heavy for the ancient Mariner hath been accorded to the Polar Spirit, who returneth southward.

The other was a softer voice,
As soft as honey-dew:
Quoth he, 'The man hath penance done,
And penance more will do.'"

PART SIX

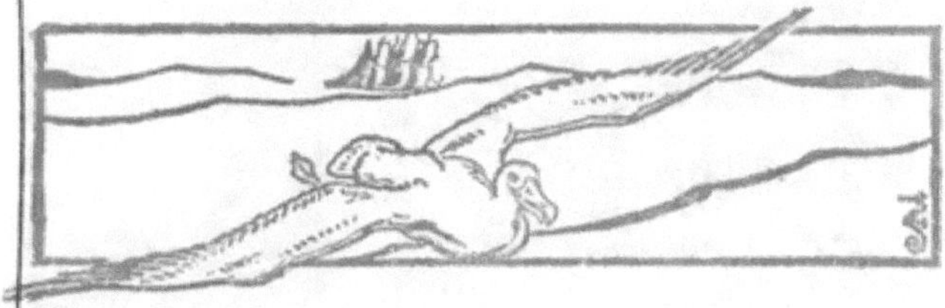

PART VI.

FIRST VOICE.

'BVT tell me, tell me!
speak again,
Thy soft response
renewing—
What makes that ship drive on
so fast?
What is the ocean doing?'

SECOND VOICE.

'Still as a slave before his lord,
The ocean hath no blast;

His great bright eye most si-
lently
Up to the moon is cast—

If he may know which way to
go;
For she guides him smooth or
grim.
See, brother, see! how graciously
She looketh down on him.'

The Mariner hath been cast into a trance; for the angelic power causeth the vessel to drive northward faster than human life could endure.

FIRST VOICE.

'But why drives on that ship so
fast,
Without or wave or wind?'

SECOND VOICE.

'The air is cut away before,
And closes from behind.

Fly, brother, fly! more high,
more high!
Or we shall be belated:
For slow and slow that ship
will go,
When the Mariner's trance is
abated.'

I woke, and we were sailing on
As in a gentle weather:
'T was night, calm night, the
moon was high;
The dead men stood together.

The supernatural motion is retarded; the Mariner awakes, and his penance begins anew.

All stood together on the deck,
For a charnel-dungeon fitter:

All fixed on me their stony eyes,
That in the moon did glitter.

The pang, the curse, with which
they died,
Had never passed away:
I could not draw my eyes from
theirs,
Nor turn them up to pray.

The curse is finally expiated.

And now this spell was snapt: once more
I viewed the ocean green,
And looked far north, yet little
saw
Of what had else been seen—

Like one, that on a lonesome road
Doth walk in fear and dread,
And having once turned round, walks on,
And turns no more his head;
Because he knows, a frightful fiend
Doth close behind him tread.

But soon there breathed a wind on me,
Nor sound nor motion made:
Its path was not upon the sea,
In ripple or in shade.

It raised my hair, it fanned my
cheek
Like a meadow-gale of spring—
It mingled strangely with my
fears,
Yet it felt like a welcoming.

Swiftly, swiftly flew the ship,
Yet she sailed softly too:
Sweetly, sweetly blew the
breeze—
On me alone it blew.

And the ancient Mariner beholdeth his native country.

Oh! dream of joy! is this indeed
The lighthouse top I see?
Is this the hill? is this the kirk?
Is this my own countree?

We drifted o'er the harbor-bar,
And I with sobs did pray—
O let me be awake, my God!
Or let me sleep alway.

The harbor-bay was clear as glass,
So smoothly it was strewn!
And on the bay the moonlight
lay,
And the shadow of the moon.

The rock shone bright, the kirk
no less,
That stands above the rock:
The moonlight steeped in si-
lentness
The steady weathercock.

And the bay was white with
silent light
Till, rising from the same,
Full many shapes, that shadows
were,
In crimson colors came.

The angelic spirits leave the dead bodies.

A little distance from the prow
Those crimson shadows were :
I turned my eyes upon the
deck—
O Christ! what saw I there!

And appear in their own forms of light.

Each corse lay flat, lifeless and
flat,
And, by the holy rood!
A man all light, a seraph-man,
On every corse there stood.

This seraph-band, each waved
his hand:
It was a heavenly sight!
They stood as signals to the land,
Each one a lovely light;

This seraph-band, each waved
his hand,
No voice did they impart—
No voice; but oh! the silence
sank
Like music on my heart.

But soon I heard the dash of
oars,
I heard the Pilot's cheer;

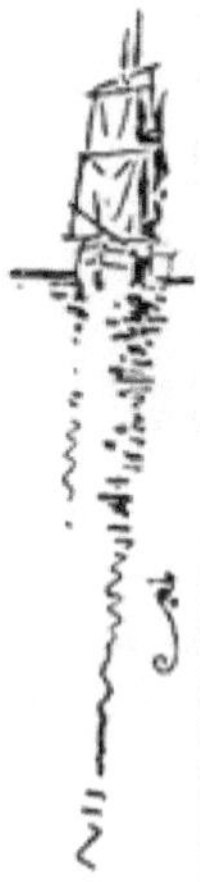

My head was turned perforce
away,
And I saw a boat appear.

The Pilot and the Pilot's boy,
I heard them coming fast:
Dear Lord in Heaven! it was a
joy
The dead men could not blast.

I saw a third—I heard his voice:
It is the Hermit good!
He singeth loud his godly hymns
That he makes in the wood.
He 'll shrieve my soul, he 'll
wash away
The Albatross's blood."

PART SEVEN

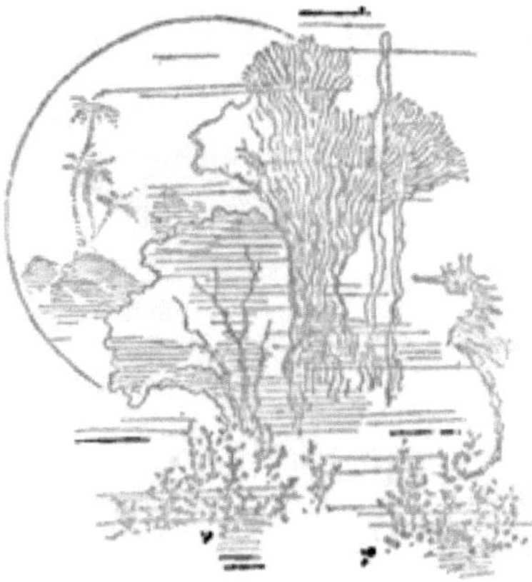

PART VII.

The Hermit of the wood,

THIS Hermit good lives in that wood
Which slopes down to the sea.
How loudly his sweet voice he rears!
He loves to talk with marineres
That come from a far countree.

He kneels at morn, and noon, and eve—
He hath a cushion plump:

It is the moss that wholly hides
The rotted old oak-stump.

The skiff-boat neared: I heard
them talk
'Why, this is strange, I trow!
Where are those lights so many
and fair,
That signal made but now?'

Approach-eth the ship with wonder.

'Strange, by my faith!' the
Hermit said—
'And they answered not our
cheer!
The planks looked warped! and
see those sails,
How thin they are and sere!

I never saw aught like to them,
Unless perchance it were
Brown skeletons of leaves that
lag
My forest-brook along;
When the ivy-tod is heavy with
snow,
And the owlet whoops to the
wolf below,
That eats the she-wolf's young.'

'Dear Lord! it hath a fiendish
look—
(The Pilot made reply)
I am a-feared'—'Push on,
push on!'
Said the Hermit cheerily.

The boat came closer to the
ship,
But I nor spake nor stirred;
The boat came close beneath
the ship,
And straight a sound was heard.

The ship suddenly sinketh.

Under the water it rumbled on,
Still louder and more dread:
It reached the ship, it split the
bay;
The ship went down like lead.

The ancient Mariner is saved in the Pilot's boat.

Stunned by the loud and dread-
ful sound,
Which sky and ocean smote,

Like one that hath been seven
days drowned
My body lay afloat;
But swift as dreams, myself I
found
Within the Pilot's boat.

Upon the whirl, where sank the
ship,
The boat spun round & round;
And all was still, save that the
hill
Was telling of the sound.

I moved my lips— the Pilot
shrieked
And fell down in a fit;

The holy Hermit raised his eyes,
And prayed where he did sit.

I took the oars: the Pilot's boy,
Who now doth crazy go,
Laughed loud and long, and
all the while
His eyes went to and fro.
'Ha! ha!' quoth he, 'full plain
I see,
The Devil knows how to row.'

And now, all in my own
countree,
I stood on the firm land!
The Hermit stepped forth from
the boat,
And scarcely he could stand.

'O shrieve me, shrieve me, holy
man!'
The Hermit crossed his brow.
'Say quick,' quoth he, 'I bid
thee say—
What manner of man art thou?'

The ancient Mariner earnestly entreateth the Hermit to shrieve him; and the penance of life falls on him.

Forthwith this frame of mine
was wrenched
With a woful agony,
Which forced me to begin my
tale;
And then it left me free.

Since then, at an uncertain hour,
That agony returns:
And till my ghastly tale is told,
This heart within me burns.

And ever and anon throughout his future life an agony constraineth him to travel from land to land.

I pass, like night, from land to
 land;
I have strange power of speech;
That moment that his face I see,
I know the man that must hear
 me:
To him my tale I teach.

What loud uproar bursts from
 that door!
The wedding-guests are there:
But in the garden-bower the
 bride
And bride-maids singing are:
And hark the little vesper bell,
Which biddeth me to prayer!

O Wedding-Guest! this soul
hath been
Alone on a wide, wide sea:
So lonely 't was, that God him-
self
Scarce seemed there to be.

O sweeter than the marriage-
feast,
'T is sweeter far to me,
To walk together to the kirk
With a goodly company!—

To walk together to the kirk,
And all together pray,
While each to his great Father
blends,

Old men, and babes, and lov-
ing friends,
And youths and maidens gay!

And to teach by own example love and reverence to all things that God made and loveth.

Farewell! farewell! but this I
tell
To thee, thou Wedding-Guest!
He prayeth well, who loveth well
Both man and bird and beast.

He prayeth best, who loveth best
All things both great and small;
For the dear God who loveth us,
He made and loveth all."

The Mariner, whose eye is bright,
Whose beard with age is hoar,

Is gone: and now the Wedding-
Guest
Turned from the bridegroom's
door.

He went like one that hath
been stunned,
And is of sense forlorn:
A sadder and a wiser man,
He rose the morrow morn.

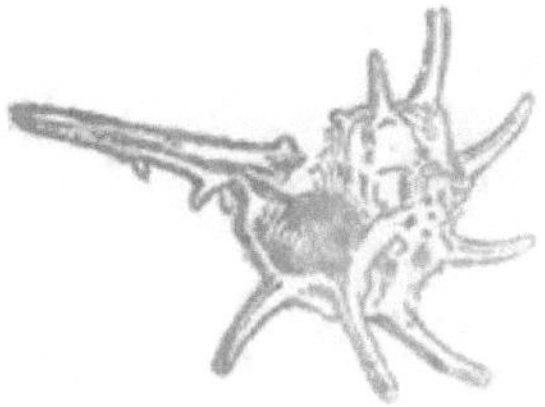

SO here endeth the *RIME OF THE ANCIENT MARINER*, by SAMUEL TAYLOR COLERIDGE, as done into a book by the *Roycrofters* at the *Roycroft Shop* that is in East Aurora, Erie County, New York, U. S. A. Completed this 15th day May, Anno Christi, MDCCCXCIX

ROYCROFT

ELBERT HUBBARD

www.ingramcontent.com/pod-product-compliance
Lightning Source LLC
Chambersburg PA
CBHW032204010726
47493CB00008BA/2819
* 9 7 8 3 3 3 7 1 7 4 7 4 3 *